zenda

A New Dimension

For:
Molly & GiGi
Johnny & Gena
Frances & James

Thank you to:
Birdie for divine inspiration.
Barbara B. for giving life to Persuaja.
Mom and Dad for everything.
Pam Amodeo, Maryann Wheaton,
and Blue Digital for supernatural covers.
Caspar & Charlotte for their magic
at Amodeo Petti.
Broadthink for professional guidance.

zenda

A New Dimension

created by
Ken Petti and John Amodeo

written with
Cassandra Westwood

Grosset & Dunlap • New York

Copyright © 2004 by Ken Petti & John Amodeo. All rights reserved.
Published by Grosset & Dunlap, a division of Penguin Young Readers Group, 345 Hudson Street, New York, New York 10014.
GROSSET & DUNLAP is a trademark of Penguin Group (USA) Inc.
Printed in the U.S.A.

Library of Congress Cataloging-in-Publication Data is available.

ISBN 0-448-43254-4   A B C D E F G H I J

Contents

I am in so much trouble!

It all started the day before my gazing ball ceremony. Here on Azureblue, everyone gets a gazing ball when they're twelve. Each ball reveals thirteen musings—they're like little bits of wisdom and inspiration that help you on life's journey.

Well, I couldn't wait to get my gazing ball, so I snuck in a day early to see mine. And I sort of . . . broke it.

I thought I was in trouble then. But things got worse. Alexandra White, a girl from school, told me about a ritual to put my gazing ball back together. To do the ritual, I had to steal a dangerous orchid from my parents' greenhouse.

I didn't think they'd even know it was missing.

But then everything got out of control. I had to stop the ritual and take the orchid back to my parents. That's when I really got in trouble.

Things aren't all bad. I did find one piece of my missing gazing ball. I got my first musing, too: <u>'Every flower blooms in its own time.'</u> I learned a lot about being patient when I got my first musing. But I still have a lot to learn . . .

Twelve pieces of my gazing ball are missing. I asked Persuaja, a pretty powerful psychic, when I would find them. She wouldn't tell me what my future looks like, but she gave me one hint.

Persuaja said I would bind my next musing in another dimension. I had no idea what she meant . . . and then one day, my whole world changed completely!

You'll see what I mean. It wasn't easy, but things got back to normal. Well, as normal as things can be when you're a girl growing up on Azureblue!

Cosmically yours,
Zenda

———⸺⸺———

⟨⟨⟨⟩⟩⟩

Nothing But Trouble

⟨⟨⟨⟩⟩⟩

A blue-bellied fly buzzed across the fields of Azureblue Karmaceuticals. A few feet away, the long, green stem of a nashera plant gently bent toward the fly, as though it was following the sound. The plant's yellow, pod-shaped flower opened up, and a pale green mist floated out into the morning air.

The fly hovered in midair for a second, then flew directly toward the mist. It flew right into the pod, which suddenly snapped shut. The plant stem bent back to its original position, and then stopped.

Zenda watched the scene from the edge of the nashera patch. She cringed when the fly disappeared. Then she sighed and resumed pulling weeds from the brown dirt.

She knew her parents were upset with her, but she never guessed Verbena and Vetiver could be *this* upset. Weeding the nashera patch was one of the worst jobs in the whole field. Zenda had never had to do it before.

But Vetiver had been firm. "Nashera plants play a valuable role on Azureblue," he reminded her. Zenda's father loved to lecture her about the importance of plants. "They are nature's way of controlling damaging insect pests. The planet's farmers depend on them to grow our food."

"Couldn't I harvest some rose petals instead?" Zenda had asked hopefully. She'd much rather risk thorn scratches than watch the nashera at work.

But Vetiver had been firm, and Zenda didn't argue. Deep down, she knew her parents had every right to be upset with her. After all, she *had* stolen an azura orchid—a flower with such dangerous powers it had to be kept under lock and key.

For the past week, Zenda had been playing the events of that night over and over in her mind. It had all started when Zenda decided to sneak a peek at her gazing ball the night before the big gazing ball ceremony.

Every girl and boy on Azureblue received a gazing ball before her or his thirteenth birthday. Usually, a student would study her gazing ball. The ball would slowly reveal thirteen musings, which would help her face the challenges of becoming an adult. After she studied all thirteen musings, the gazing ball would reveal what special gift she possessed.

That's what usually happened. But when Zenda snuck in to see her gazing ball, she dropped it and broke it. Then Alexandra White had told Zenda of a ritual she could use to put her gazing ball back together. To do it, Zenda would need to steal an azura orchid.

Zenda was desperate to get her gazing ball back, so she had stolen the orchid. And that hadn't solved anything. The ritual had been a disaster, and her gazing ball was still in pieces. She had told her parents about stealing the orchid—and had spent all her spare time helping with the plants as a result.

4

A fly buzzed past Zenda's face, and she quickly moved back. The green mist produced by the nashera smelled great to blue-bellied flies and potato bugs, but it smelled awful to Zenda. She quickly covered her nose with her hand.

Zenda had felt a bad mood coming on all morning, and now it had arrived. Making her work in the nashera patch was just mean! It was a beautiful, sunny morning. She could be swimming in Crystal Creek with Camille. But, instead, she was stuck here . . .

Three small black flower petals floated down in front of Zenda's face. She frowned again. This morning, she had woven stems of midnight violets into a flower crown to wear on her head. Now they were withering in response to her bad mood.

"Why doesn't this happen to anybody else but me?" Zenda complained to the nashera plants. It was rare for anyone to show signs of their special gift before turning thirteen, but Zenda already had the gift of *kani*—the ability to communicate with plants. They responded to her mood, whether she was happy, sad—or grumpy, like today.

Most people would be happy to have such a gift, and Zenda liked it—sometimes. Most of the time, though, she couldn't control it, and strange things happened, especially to the flower crown she wore every day. Most girls wore perfect crowns of white daisies or miniature roses. But Zenda's crowns were always sprouting thorns or changing colors. Alexandra loved to tease her about it.

"It's not fair!" Zenda moaned again, and a nearby nashera plant responded by spraying her with smelly green mist.

"That's it!" Zenda cried. "Forget about the weeds. I'm going to pull out every last one of you by your roots!"

The whole patch responded with a shower of mist. Zenda quickly backed up.

"I can't take this anymore!" she yelled.

She started stomping back to the house when she noticed a small brown dog running across the fields, heading toward her. Zenda knelt down, and the dog bounded into her lap, licking her face.

"Good boy, Oscar," Zenda said, scratching behind his ears. A tiny paper envelope dangled from a piece of string tied to his collar. Zenda untied the envelope, opened it up, and read the tiny note inside.

Zenda,
I miss you! I can't wait until the Project Fair this afternoon. What dress are you wearing? I'm wearing my new blue one with the butterflies on it.
See you soon!
Camille

Zenda smiled. These days, Zenda had been so busy, she barely saw her best friend.

Luckily, Camille lived close by, so Zenda's dog Oscar had become their courier, traveling back and forth with messages they sent to each other. Oscar seemed to enjoy it, although Zenda knew it was probably because of the homemade cookies Camille's mother made for him.

Seeing Cam was the only reason Zenda was excited about going to the Project Fair. In a few hours, students from the Cobalt School for Girls and the Cobalt School for Boys would present their school projects to the village elders. It was a yearly tradition. Every twelve-year-old student in Azureblue got to study the subject of his or her choice in depth for an entire year.

Zenda had chosen the thirteen planets in Azureblue's solar system. She loved the idea of traveling to faraway places like her grandmother had, and studying the planets made them feel so much closer. Camille, of course, had chosen insects. She loved anything with six legs, whether it crept, crawled, stung, or flew. The projects weren't finished yet, but the elders liked to check on their progress in the first part of the year.

Normally, Zenda would have been excited to go. But things hadn't been the same since the azura orchid. Alexandra White had told everyone that Zenda had snitched on her. She was really angry. And when Alex got angry, well . . . you didn't want to be in her way.

Zenda sighed and looked down at her dress. It had once been bright blue, but it had faded to a streaky gray after repeated wash-ings. Dirt covered her feet, and her crown of violets had just about fallen apart.

"If I'm going to go, I might as well look good. Right, Oscar?" she said.

Oscar gave a little bark and jumped off her lap. Zenda stood up, grabbed the wheel-barrow full of weeds, and pushed it up the hill. She dumped the weeds into the compost heap and then headed into the bright green house. Verbena and Vetiver were working in one of the greenhouses, so she had the place to herself.

Zenda picked up Oscar. "I'm going to take a bath," she said. "Do you want one, too?"

Oscar whined and wriggled out of Zenda's arms. She laughed and headed upstairs.

An hour later, she stood in front of the mirror in her bedroom. She wore her new purple dress—her favorite color. She had brushed her long, red hair until it shone. Around her neck she wore a small, purple silk pouch, hanging from a cord.

She stared at herself for a moment. Her blue eyes stared right back at her.

"Something's missing," she muttered.

Of course! Her flower crown. Zenda pulled some purple coneflowers out of a vase on her dresser. She expertly twisted them into a wreath and placed the crown on her head.

"Perfect!" Zenda said. The flowers matched her dress exactly. She started for the door, then stopped.

"Just one more thing."

Azureblue Karmaceuticals, the company owned by Zenda's parents, made hundreds of products. Bottles of lotions and potions covered Zenda's dresser. She thought for a minute, then picked one from the bunch.

The label read *Relaxation*. It was just what Zenda needed. She needed to relax, have a good time at the fair, and not worry about Alexandra. She dabbed some of the elixir on her wrists and inhaled the scent. The sweet lavender and peppery basil made her feel calmer instantly.

"All right then," Zenda told her reflection. "It's now or never!"

Before she left, Zenda walked to the greenhouses. The two glass buildings had curved roofs and held plants too delicate to grow out in the open. One of the buildings had a separate room filled with plant presses, glass beakers, and other tools used for turning plants into oils, lotions, and other products. That's where Zenda found her parents.

"Zenda, you look lovely!" Verbena exclaimed.

Zenda's mother set down a bottle of pale blue liquid and walked up to Zenda, giving her a hug. Zenda was almost as tall as Verbena now, but other than that, they didn't look much alike. Verbena had long, brown hair that fell to her waist, and eyes the color of honey.

Her father's hazel eyes twinkled behind his glasses. "You look awfully nice for someone who's been with the nashera all morning," Vetiver said. "Are you sure you got all of the weeds?"

Zenda frowned. "I got all I could before those little beasts started attacking me."

Vetiver shook his head. "I suppose you

can finish them tomorrow," he said. "But you can't let them get the better of you, Zenda. They're very important to—"

"I know!" Zenda didn't usually interrupt, but she couldn't bear to hear one of her father's lectures again. "Besides, I had to get ready for the Project Fair."

Vetiver's stern expression changed. "How could I forget? We just delivered a beautiful flower arrangement there this morning."

"Have a good time, Zenda," Verbena said. "But remember, when it's over—"

"I'll come right home," Zenda finished for her. She still had another week of restriction before her life would be back to normal.

Zenda kissed both of her parents and left the greenhouse. Then she headed down the path into the village.

The Project Fair would be held at the Cobalt School for Boys. That meant Mykal would be there. Thinking about seeing Mykal made Zenda nervous all over again. She breathed deeply, inhaling the Relaxation Elixir.

She and Mykal had been friends forever. Lately, Zenda had been wishing that they could be more than just friends someday. But since she had stolen the orchid, he had been distant. He spent his spare time working for Zenda's parents, and whenever they bumped into each other, he mumbled an excuse and ran away.

He must think I'm terrible, Zenda had convinced herself. Who wouldn't? Stealing the orchid was a terrible thing to do.

Zenda took another deep breath. Everything would be fine. She would find Camille, and they would stand in a corner somewhere and no one would bother them.

The path opened up into the Commons Circle, a round park in the center of the village. All of the paths in the village began here (or ended here, depending on which direction you were going), and spiraled out like spokes on a wheel.

The circle was crowded with boys and girls heading for the Project Fair. They stood in small groups, talking and laughing.

In the very center of the circle stood a tall girl wearing a crown of red roses. She wore a long dress that matched the color of her shiny chestnut hair. She was surrounded by girls from Zenda's class.

Zenda stopped. She wasn't in the mood to see Alexandra right now. She headed toward the edge of the circle, as far away from Alex as she could get.

She had almost made it across when a sharp voice pierced the air.

"Well look who it is," Alexandra said. "It's Zenda the snitch!"

Zenda on Fire

Zenda felt her face flush with embarrassment. Usually, ignoring Alexandra was the safest thing to do, so she just kept walking. Alexandra and her friends erupted into giggles as she walked past.

Zenda was so flustered that she didn't even notice Camille standing in front of her. She practically bumped into her friend.

"Zenda, are you okay? Your face is bright red," Camille said.

"Sorry," Zenda replied. "It's just—"

Zenda didn't have to finish, because Camille understood right away. She grabbed Zenda's arm.

"Come on, let's get to the school," she said. "I'm sure Alex won't give you any trouble in front of the elders."

Every year, nine elders were chosen to hold positions of honor in the village. They kept things running smoothly, making sure the roads were safe, that the village stayed clean—and that students were learning what they

17

were supposed to. The Project Fair was a chance for students to show off their talents, and for the elders to check in on the students.

Just being near Camille made Zenda feel better. Camille had skin the color of a chestnut, curly black hair, and large brown eyes. She was wearing the blue dress she had told Zenda about in the note.

"I helped my mom make it," Camille said proudly as they walked. Camille's mother was a talented dressmaker who owned a shop in the village. "I think it came out pretty good."

"It's better than good. It's great!" Zenda said.

"You look great, too," Camille complimented. "Those red flowers go nicely with your purple dress. What kind are they?"

Red flowers? Zenda groaned. She lifted the flower crown off her head. The purple coneflowers had changed to a brilliant red.

"They must have changed when I got embarrassed," Zenda said. "Why does this keep happening?!"

Before Camille could reply, the Cobalt School for Boys came into view. The school looked a lot like the girls' school that Zenda and Camille attended. Four U-shaped buildings were arranged to form a circle. In the center of the circle grew a towering, ancient oak tree.

Crowds of girls and boys were gathered in front of a building with the image of a maple tree carved into its wooden door. Zenda had visited the Maple Building yesterday, when they had taken their projects to be put on display.

"Look!" Camille said, nudging her. "There's Mykal!"

Mykal stood next to the door, talking with three other boys. His shaggy blond hair hung over his eyes, like it always did. He wore a dark green shirt and brown pants.

Zenda knew he liked to wear green because it reminded him of plants, his favorite thing in the world. Zenda always noticed that green matched the brilliant emerald color of his eyes.

"Let's go say hi," Camille said.

"I don't know," Zenda began, but at that moment the door to the Maple Building opened. A man dressed in flowing tan pants and a white shirt stepped out. His dark black hair was cut short and neatly combed.

It was Wei Lan, the headmaster of the Cobalt School for Boys. Zenda loved her school, but she had always thought the boys were much luckier than the girls in one way. Wei Lan was gentle and kind, with a friendly smile—the opposite of Magenta White, the headmistress of the girls' school.

"Please enter the building quietly and respectfully," Wei Lan told the gathered students. "The elders are waiting for you."

The students filed into the Maple Building, some speaking in nervous and excited whispers. Zenda and Camille entered right behind Mykal.

Tables had been set up all along the walls of the building. Sculptures, plants, stacks of papers, and other projects were arranged neatly on the tables.

A huge arrangement of living flowers grew from a green clay pot in the center of the room. Zenda recognized some of the rarest flowers from her parents' greenhouse. Tall stalks of firebrush flowers rose from the center of the pot. Their red flowers looked like large pom-poms. Verbena had surrounded them with deep purple irises and dark green grass.

The nine village elders stood around the flowers. They all wore white robes, and most had hair the same color. They greeted the students with warm smiles.

A woman stepped out from the group. Zenda knew her. Mari had been a good friend of her grandmother's. Zenda remembered

Delphina and Mari taking her for walks in the woods when she was a little girl.

"We are looking forward to seeing your projects," she said. "I hope you enjoy sharing one another's work, as well."

"Let's go find our projects," Zenda told Camille. Zenda had worked hard on the first part of her year-long project, a detailed diagram of the solar system. She hoped the elders would be impressed.

But before Zenda could take a step, she felt a tap on her shoulder. She turned around to see Alexandra.

"What do you want, Alex?" she snapped.

"I wanted to say I'm sorry for calling you a snitch before," Alexandra said.

Zenda didn't believe it for a second. "Really?"

"Yes," Alexandra said, a smug smile on her face. "I'm sorry for calling you a snitch. I should have called you a snitch *and* a thief!"

Two girls standing behind Alexandra laughed. Gena and Astrid followed Alexandra everywhere—and agreed with everything the popular girl said.

Zenda had been ignoring Alexandra all week. But she couldn't take it anymore.

"Just stop it, Alex!" she said, her voice rising. "Stealing the orchid was your idea, not mine. I'm sorry I went along with it."

Alexandra scowled. "So now you're a liar, too?"

That did it. "I'm not lying!" Zenda yelled. "And anyone who believes you has the brains of a bullfrog!"

The room went quiet. Zenda felt every face turn in her direction.

"Come on, Zenda," Camille said quietly. She tugged on Zenda's arm.

But a sudden sound made Zenda jump. She turned around.

A hissing, popping sound was coming from the firebrush flowers. Zenda went pale.

She had seen this happen once before. When exposed to extreme heat, the flowers had a strange reaction.

"Oh, no," Zenda whispered. Then she raised her voice. "Everybody back!"

But her warning came too late. Sizzling orange sparks flew off the firebrush flowers like a mini display of fireworks. The sparks flew into the crowd, stinging anyone they touched. Students squealed as they pushed one another to get out of the way.

"What is going on here?" one of the elders asked, walking up to Zenda.

Mari grabbed his arm. "Arthur, this is Zenda," she said. "Delphina's granddaughter. The one with the gift."

Alexandra smirked. "Zenda's always doing things like this," she said in a prim voice. "She can't keep her gift under control at all. It's very disruptive to our learning."

Mari gave Zenda a sympathetic look, but Zenda didn't see it. All she could see was a swarm of faces. Some looked at her disapprovingly, shaking their heads. Some were laughing and pointing. Even Mykal.

Zenda's stomach felt hollow.

"I've got to go," she whispered to Camille.

Then she ran.

The Hawthorn Grove

Zenda ran out the door, past the oak tree and onto the path. Then she veered to the right, stepping into the stand of trees that marked the edge of the Western Woods. She knew Camille would try to follow her, and she didn't want to see anyone right now. She wanted to be alone.

Zenda's feet pounded on the mossy ground as she ran, not caring where she was headed. When she couldn't run any farther, she sank down at the base of an elm tree.

She closed her eyes and took deep breaths. Her heart beat quickly in her chest. When she opened her eyes again, she leaned her head back and looked up. The green leaves of the trees in the woods formed a huge canopy overhead, letting in only slivers of sunlight here and there. Zenda suddenly felt a chill. She wrapped her arms around her chest.

It wasn't fair. Alexandra had started it all. She had made Zenda angry, and the firebrush flowers had sensed the heat of her anger. She hadn't done it on purpose.

And now the elders had seen Zenda's ability for themselves.

They must think I'm some kind of freak, Zenda worried. *It's bad enough I can't go to gazing ball class with the others. The elders will probably ban me from the school for good.*

Zenda nervously fingered the silk pouch she wore around her neck. She had started wearing the pouch in case she found another piece of her gazing ball. The first piece she had found was a shard of glass that had appeared magically out of the air. Zenda wanted to be prepared in case that happened again.

She also kept something else in the pouch. Zenda loosened the strings and took out a small lavender card.

Persuaja's card. Zenda had met the mysterious psychic the night she had stolen the azura orchid. Persuaja had saved her from the orchid's dangerous powers.

She had also been kind. Persuaja told

Zenda that she would get back the pieces of her gazing ball, although she would not tell Zenda how. But she had given Zenda one clue about her next musing.

"It can't be found in this dimension," Persuaja had said.

Zenda had turned those words over and over since that night. What could they possibly mean? Now, sitting in the shade of the woods, the mysterious words annoyed her. Nothing had gone right since the night she had stolen the orchid. Persuaja seemed so sure of the future, but to Zenda, things looked bleak.

She wanted answers. Now.

The card said that Persuaja lived in the Western Woods, inside the Hawthorn Grove. Zenda had visited the grove many times on her walks with Delphina, but never imagined that anyone lived there.

She stood up and tried to get her bearings. A shallow stream—a long, skinny arm that snaked off of Crystal Creek—ran through the woods and led to the grove. If she found the stream, finding Persuaja would be easy.

The trouble was, Zenda had run into the woods without thinking. She frowned. Then she listened.

If she held her breath, she could just make out the sound of the running stream. She quickly headed toward the noise.

She soon found herself on the bank of the shallow, rocky stream. Even in the dim light, Zenda could see the smooth pebbles on the stream's bottom. Clear water cascaded over the rocks.

The grove was upstream, Zenda knew, so she headed that way, keeping close to the bank. She walked that way for about twenty minutes when the Hawthorn Grove came into sight.

Zenda had always been fascinated by the hawthorns. They were more like bushes, really, and grew to be about twice as tall as Zenda herself. Today, tiny white flowers dotted the dark green leaves; Zenda knew they would become clusters of bright red berries soon.

The hawthorns in the grove grew in a perfect circle. Zenda had never imagined that there was anything inside the circle, much less the home of a woman with psychic powers. But how was she supposed to get in? The hawthorns grew together thickly, and sharp thorns covered the branches. She couldn't push her way through.

Zenda walked around the circle, looking for an entrance. She had gone about halfway when she found one. A curved archway, just tall enough for her to pass through, had been trimmed out of the trees. Zenda did not remember seeing it before, but it was a way in. She stepped inside the circle.

A small stone cottage sat in the very center of the grove. The gray stone blocks looked as though they had been put together ages ago, but the thatched straw roof looked clean and new. From what Zenda could see, small plots of herbs and flowers grew all around the cottage. They looked tall, green, and healthy; Zenda briefly wondered how they could grow so well in so little sunlight.

The cottage looked simple, like it might belong to anyone in the village — except for the door. A large eye had been carved into the dark wood. Zenda recognized the eye from Persuaja's card. She stepped up to the door and knocked.

There was no response. Zenda knocked a second time, and the door slowly pushed open at her touch. The sound of tinkling chimes rang through the cottage as she stepped inside.

Zenda gasped. The inside of the cottage was anything but simple. It didn't look like anything she had ever seen before.

Bundles of dried herbs hung from the

ceiling rafters, along with shimmering crystals tied to strings. Tall bookcases lined every inch of wall space that Zenda could see. Some of the shelves held rows and rows of books. One was crowded with glass bottles filled with brightly-colored liquids. Another shelf held huge rocks and crystals. Some of them looked familiar, but others—like the jagged spire that seemed to glow a pale green—must have come from somewhere else besides Azureblue.

An overstuffed couch the color of a ripe eggplant faced the front door. On the floor in front of it was a round lavender rug with the eye design woven into it. Beyond the couch, Zenda could see a second room that looked like a kitchen.

"Persuaja?" Zenda called out. This had to be the right place. She stepped through the front room and walked to the back room, which held an iron stove, a wooden table and chairs, and more dried herbs, but no Persuaja.

Then Zenda noticed a door against the

right wall. Thick purple curtains covered the doorway.

"Persuaja?" she called again. No one answered. She pulled aside the curtains and stepped in.

The room was dark, except for the light of candles coming from a small, round table. Persuaja sat at the table, her head down. She didn't seem to notice Zenda at all.

Zenda hesitated, afraid to startle the woman. She had forgotten how imposing Persuaja looked. Even sitting down, you could see what a tall woman she was. Her long, black hair cascaded down her back. She wore a black dress with long sleeves. Crystals and amulets—too many to count at a glance—dangled from chains she wore around her neck.

Zenda was about to turn around when Persuaja suddenly looked up.

Her eyes locked with Zenda's. Zenda had not forgotten them. They were deep black, tinged with blue, reminding

Zenda of a night sky.

"I am sorry, Zenda," she said. "I heard you come in earlier, and I sensed it was you, but I did not want to break my concentration. Please, sit down."

Persuaja motioned to a chair opposite hers. As Zenda sat down, she saw what Persuaja had been looking at. On the table in front of her was a black bowl filled with water.

"What are you doing?" Zenda asked, suddenly curious.

"Scrying," Persuaja said. "Images may form in the water if my mind is clear and my intentions are good. I am hoping to find something. Something important."

Zenda looked at Persuaja expectantly.

"When something unusual happens on the astral plane, a psychic will sense it," Persuaja explained. "If you remember, that is how I knew you had stolen the azura orchid."

She said the last sentence without any judgment in her voice, yet Zenda still cringed to be reminded of it.

"I remember," Zenda said.

"This morning, I sensed another disturbance," Persuaja continued. "A sudden windstorm picked up several villages away. But the storm is unnatural."

"You mean magical?" Zenda asked.

Persuaja nodded. "The windstorm itself is not a problem. But it carries with it something dangerous. Tempus seeds."

The word sounded familiar to Zenda. She knew she had heard it in botany class before.

"Isn't it a classified plant?" Zenda asked. "My parents aren't even licensed to grow it."

"Only one person on Azureblue is licensed to handle the seeds. The effects of the fully grown plant are only legendary, because the plant has not grown for hundreds of years," Persuaja explained. "Yet I have heard something of its power. If it blooms, the plant could alter life as we know it on Azureblue. Forever."

Persuaja said the word in a deep, dramatic tone, and Zenda shuddered. Still, she was confused. "If it's so dangerous, why are the seeds still kept? Why weren't they destroyed?"

The psychic shook her head. "You know yourself how much plants are valued here on this planet. None of the elders could bear to destroy them. Scientists have been studying the seeds, trying to see if they can control their power. But the windstorm set them free. I sense that it is possible that the seeds themselves caused the storm to rise. Nothing that is meant to grow can stand to be locked up for very long."

"But if the seeds are loose, the plants could grow again," Zenda said, understanding the urgency of the situation. "What can you do?"

"I am trying to scry their location," Persuaja said. "I was quite close, until you entered. But I sensed there is an important reason you came here today."

Zenda's fascination with the tempus seeds evaporated as the scene at the Project Fair came flooding back to her.

"Everything's going wrong," Zenda said. "I haven't found another musing. Everyone at school thinks I'm terrible for stealing the orchid. And today I made some firebrush flowers explode all over the village elders. I can't go back there!"

"It all sounds very difficult," Persuaja said sympathetically.

"I want to know what's going to happen," Zenda blurted out. "I know you said I had to find out on my own. But it's too hard. If I knew how everything was going to work out, things would be so much easier!"

Persuaja shook her head. "Zenda, dear, the future is always changing," she said. "I could look in my crystal and tell you exactly how to get the rest of your musings, but that's not how it works. You will have to learn the lessons of your musings for yourself. If you try to take a shortcut, the musings will only change on you."

Zenda felt like crying. "But can't you tell me if Alexandra is ever going to stop attacking me? Or if the elders are going to ban me from school? That's not cheating, is it?"

Persuaja sighed. "Those experiences are all part of your journey, Zenda," she said. Then she looked thoughtful. "Although, I suppose I could—"

The sound of chimes rang through the cottage. Persuaja frowned. "Most likely it's that fool from the village wanting to know if the girl next door is in love with him," she said. "I will dispose of him quickly. I must find those seeds!"

Persuaja hurried from the room, leaving Zenda sulking in her chair. As her eyes adjusted to the darkness, she looked around the small room.

The walls were painted a purple so dark it was almost black. Besides the table and chairs, there was a side table made of dark wood that shone in the candlelight. On top of the table, a black velvet cloth covered an unusually-shaped object.

Zenda felt a chill of excitement. It had to be Persuaja's crystal pyramid. She stood up and lifted the velvet cloth.

Underneath was a clear crystal with a wide, square base that reached a point at the top. It reflected the flickering candlelight in the room, as well as Zenda's own face. Zenda couldn't help taking a closer look. Persuaja could see the future inside this crystal, but she wouldn't do it for Zenda.

What do you have to show me? Zenda silently asked the shimmering stone.

The candlelight danced inside the pyramid. As Zenda watched, the flames came together to form a shape. The shape became more and more distinct.

Zenda gasped.

There was an image inside the crystal. It was Persuaja. But she looked ghostly pale, and her eyes were pale and filled with terror.

Zenda watched as Persuaja's image transformed. Her face turned a cold gray, the color of stone. Then, suddenly, violently, the image shattered into millions of grains of fine powder. The powder swirled around the inside of the crystal, and then vanished.

"Persuaja!" Zenda cried.

So Sleepy . . .

The image in the crystal horrified Zenda. She stepped back, her heart beating wildly.

What had she done? She never should have touched the crystal pyramid. She wasn't sure what the image in the crystal meant, but it looked like Persuaja was in danger. And if Zenda had put her there . . .

Her mind spinning, Zenda stumbled out of the room. She saw a back door against the kitchen wall, and for the second time that day, she ran.

Zenda ran around the grove, looking for the exit. The coneflowers on her crown, which had started as purple and then had turned red, were now white. They fell off behind her as she ran.

Why can't I do anything right? Zenda scolded herself. She couldn't face Persuaja. She couldn't go back to school. The news must have gotten back to her parents by now. She didn't want to go there, either.

Zenda had been running for a few ...es when she realized that she had veered away from the stream. Getting lost in the Western Woods would only make things worse. She quickly turned around—and tripped over a rock.

Zenda landed face-first in the dirt. Stunned and shaken, she rose to her feet.

She had fallen between two trees and found herself in a clearing. Tall evergreen trees ringed a circle of pale green grass. And thousands of snowflakes fluttered down from the sky.

Zenda blinked. She must be seeing things. It was too warm to snow in the village today. She stepped farther into the clearing and held out her hand.

Some of the snowflakes landed in her palm, but they weren't cold or wet. Zenda looked at them closely.

They weren't snowflakes at all. They were tiny black seeds surrounded by thin white fibers. They reminded Zenda of the dandelion seeds she sometimes blew into the wind, sending her wishes along with them.

Zenda twirled around, watching the seeds dance around her. They looked absolutely beautiful—like tiny fairies playing in the breeze.

The seeds seemed to respond to Zenda's delight. They swirled around her, flying faster and faster as Zenda twirled.

Then, suddenly, the seeds fell to the ground, covering the earth like a blanket.

Zenda stopped twirling. These weren't dandelion seeds. There was something odd about them . . .

The thought hit her suddenly. Tempus seeds. They had to be.

"I have to warn Persuaja," Zenda said.

But she didn't move just yet. She knelt down to examine the seeds on the ground.

They had already sprouted. Zenda watched, knowing she should get Persuaja, but some unseen force held her there. In seconds, the sprouts grew into lanky stems with oval leaves. Then a tiny white flower bud grew on the top of each stem.

All at once, the buds opened, filling the clearing with thousands of white flowers with round centers and thin, lacy petals. A scent like newly fallen snow filled the air.

Zenda found herself leaning down farther and breathing deeply. The clean scent overwhelmed her.

I should get Persuaja, Zenda told herself, but instead she sank down into the flowers, resting her head on their soft blossoms. She felt so sleepy . . .

Zenda woke to the sound of morning chimes. She quickly sat up, rubbing her eyes.

She was home, in her own bed. Her head felt strange and light.

How did I get here? Zenda wondered. She remembered the flowers growing suddenly in the clearing, and breathing in their scent, and then . . .

She must have fallen asleep. Maybe that was the strange power the tempus flowers had. Persuaja had probably followed her and brought her home.

Zenda leaned back against the pillows and sighed. Her parents must be waiting for her, wanting an explanation about the fire-brush flowers. They probably thought she had something to do with the tempus flowers, too.

Zenda reached under the covers and pulled out Luna, the doll her grandmother Delphina had passed on to her when she was just a baby. Luna's round face smiled at Zenda, like it always did. Zenda hugged the doll, inhaling the faint scent of herbs that had been stuffed into her silk body long ago.

"What am I going to do, Luna?" Zenda asked.

Sometimes, Zenda felt like a little piece

of Delphina lived on inside of Luna. She told Luna all of her problems. Sometimes, it felt like her grandmother answered her.

Before Zenda could talk to Luna, something slipped out from under her pillow. It was her journal. Zenda picked up the book, which had a purple silk cover and her name stamped on it in gold. She unclipped the pen attached to the back cover and began to write.

Yesterday was the worst day ever. Thanks to Alexandra, nobody at school likes me. The elders think I'm a freak because I made a birebrush plant explode. I went to Persuaja for help, but she said I'd have to wait and let things work out on their own.

I'm afraid to tell Persuaja about the image I saw in the crystal pyramid. What if I made that happen somehow? It was really scary. I should go back to the Hawthorn Grove and tell her. I'm sure she won't like me, either, once I do.

But first I'll probably have to weed that nasty nashera patch again. Will things ever get better??

Zenda heard a knock on the door.

"Come in," she said.

Verbena stuck her head in the room. "Zenda! Aren't you up yet? It's almost time for the festival. You'd better hurry and get dressed."

"What festival?" Zenda asked, confused.

Verbena grinned. "Don't be modest, sweetie. I'll see you downstairs in a few minutes."

Zenda climbed out of bed. The tempus flowers must have messed with her memory somehow. There was probably some festival in the village they were supposed to go to. She just hoped she had a clean dress in her closet.

Zenda felt more confused as she looked around her room. Usually, the floor was strewn with clothes and books, and the top of her dresser was filled with clutter. But she could see her face in the polished wood floor, and the bottles on her dresser were arranged in neat rows.

Another memory loss, Zenda guessed. She must have cleaned her room yesterday and forgotten about it. She walked to her closet and opened it.

She gasped. Beautiful dresses filled her closet. She recognized some from Camille's mother's shop in the village. There was no sign of the dresses that had become faded or ripped from working with the plants.

Zenda picked out a sleeveless dress the color of a spring sky. It fell gracefully to her ankles. It came with a pale pink scarf that she tied around her waist.

When she got downstairs, Verbena and Vetiver were waiting by the door.

"You look gorgeous, starshine," Vetiver said, kissing her cheek.

Verbena placed a crown of pale pink flowers on her head. "Now let's get out there. Everyone's waiting for us."

"Don't I need to finish weeding the nashera patch?" Zenda asked. She may have forgotten some things, but she knew Vetiver wanted her to finish the job.

But her father laughed. "You? Weed a nashera patch? We'd never dream of asking you to do that."

Zenda felt suddenly uneasy. Was this some kind of joke? She felt tears spring to her eyes. Verbena and Vetiver must be trying to teach her some kind of lesson.

"It wasn't my fault that the firebrush flowers exploded," she said. "Alexandra made me angry. And then I went to see Persuaja—"

Verbena shook her head. "My goodness, you are acting silly today. Now let's get outside!"

Zenda knew it was no use to argue. She followed her parents out the door.

Villagers crowded the green fields of Azureblue Karmaceuticals. Flower garlands decorated the wooden fence. Three harpists played soft music in the rose garden.

And tied between two apple trees was a large banner painted with purple letters.

"This can't be happening," Zenda whispered.

The banner read, *WE LOVE ZENDA!*

Something
Isn't Right

"Verbena, Vetiver, please," Zenda pleaded. "I don't understand."

Verbena and Vetiver exchanged glances.

"I sometimes forget how delicate you are, Zenda," Vetiver said. "You do know what day this is, don't you?"

Zenda shook her head.

"It's the day we discovered that you had the gift of *kani*, of course," he continued. "We have a festival on that day every year in your honor."

A festival? In her honor? The idea seemed ridiculous to Zenda.

Something wasn't right at all. Until she found out what it was, she decided she should play along.

"Of course," she said, trying to smile. "I had some . . . strange dreams last night. I woke up a bit confused. I just need a minute to clear my head, and I'll be right there."

"Anything you want, starshine,"

Vetiver said. Then he and Verbena walked toward the fields.

Zenda looked around the grounds, trying to take everything in. The tempus flower couldn't have messed up her mind that much, could it? She was pretty sure she would have remembered a festival like this.

And the grounds looked slightly different than she remembered. The apple orchard was on the western hill, not the eastern hill where she remembered it. And next to the rose garden was a field of tall purple coneflowers that she didn't remember being there.

Zenda looked behind her, and stopped suddenly. She was positive that her house had been painted in different shades of green, her mother's favorite color.

But this house was painted lilac with a dark purple trim. Purple was *her* favorite color. She would have remembered a purple house—wouldn't she?

Zenda turned back to the festival.

A long, wooden table had been set up in the field. It was piled high with fruit, sandwiches, and cakes. Villagers gathered around it, filling their plates. Zenda scanned the crowd.

Camille would tell her what was going on. Zenda had to find her.

But she couldn't see Camille anywhere; instead, she saw Alexandra walking toward her. Gena and Astrid followed her, as always, and the two girls could not have looked more different from each other; Gena was tall and dark; Astrid was short and pale as a lily, with white-blonde hair. But they both worshipped Alexandra.

Zenda froze. The last thing she needed was another encounter with Alex White. Alex ran to her, grabbing her by the arms.

"Come on, Zenda," she said. "It's time for the dance!"

Zenda felt herself swept up in the trio of girls. They led her toward the *WE LOVE ZENDA!* banner.

"You look amazing today, Zenda," Astrid said in her soft voice.

"Zenda looks amazing every day, Astrid," Gena corrected her.

Zenda cringed, waiting for the punch line. Alex surely had some cruel remark to add.

But nothing came. The smiles on Astrid and Gena's faces looked completely genuine.

Puzzled, Zenda let Alex and the girls lead her to a large wicker chair under the banner. Garlands of purple flowers made the chair look like some kind of throne.

"Take your seat, Zenda," Alex said. "The dancers are ready."

Zenda sat in the chair. The villagers crowded around, forming a circle. A tall woman with blonde hair entered the circle and lifted a flute to her lips. She began to play, and six young girls dressed in purple silk danced into the circle.

The girls gracefully twirled in time with the music. Their purple skirts whirled around them as they danced.

"You are so lucky, Zenda," Alex whispered in her ear. "It must be wonderful to have a dance created in your honor."

Zenda was stunned. Only the most special people in the village had dances created for them. What had Zenda done to deserve that?

The flutist stopped, and the dancers bowed and left the circle. The villagers clapped. Zenda scanned their faces, looking for Camille.

"I bet I know who you're looking for," Alex said, grinning.

"Camille," Zenda said. "Have you seen her?"

Alex laughed. "What would Camille be doing here? I meant Mykal, silly. Look, here he comes now."

Mykal made his way through the

crowd toward her. Zenda was relieved to see him. She knew Mykal would be honest with her.

Mykal wore a blue shirt the same color as Zenda's dress. He had one hand behind his back. Alex, Gena, and Astrid stepped to the side as Mykal approached.

"Mykal!" Zenda got up from her flowery throne. "I'm so glad to see you! Something strange is going on today. I need your help."

To Zenda's surprise, Mykal blushed bright red. "Hi, Zenda," he said shyly.

"Mykal, I need you to tell me what's going on here," she said impatiently.

"I have something for you," Mykal said. He took his hand out from behind his back to reveal a perfect red rose on a long stem. "I grew it just for you. It's thornless."

Now it was Zenda's turn to blush. Mykal? Giving her a flower?

She took the rose from him. "Thank you," she said softly. "It's beautiful."

Behind her, she heard Astrid gasp. "Oh, Zenda! Your crown!"

Zenda blushed deeper. Not now! She took off her crown. The pale pink flowers had turned bright red.

"No problem," Alex said. She opened a basket next to the chair. She pulled out a pink crown of flowers and placed it on Zenda's head. "There. Perfect!"

"It looks beautiful, Zenda," Mykal said, blushing again. Then he turned and darted back into the crowd.

"Mykal! Wait!" Zenda cried.

"Don't worry, he'll be back," Alex said in a teasing voice. "He follows you around like a puppy dog, doesn't he?"

Zenda sank back into the chair. Something was definitely not right. The clean bedroom. The purple house. The festival. And Alex and Mykal weren't acting like themselves at all.

It felt like some kind of dream. Like the world around her wasn't real. Almost like . . .

The next musing can't be found in this dimension, Persuaja had said.

Zenda shivered.

Maybe that's what was happening here. She was in some kind of alternate dimension—a place like her world, but different, too.

She had to find Camille right away. She had to see Persuaja.

But Zenda couldn't get away all day. All of the villagers wanted to talk to her. Verbena and Vetiver brought her a plate full of her favorite food. Alex, Gena, and Astrid never left her side.

Despite herself, Zenda started to relax.

This is what I've always wanted, Zenda realized, looking around. *Everybody likes me. Nobody thinks I'm a thief. Or a freak. Even Alexandra is being nice to me.*

Zenda looked down at the rose in her lap. She had always wished that Mykal would like her the same way she liked him. He had always seemed more interested in his plants than in Zenda. But now . . .

Zenda liked the attention. The festival lasted until the sun went down. Zenda wearily entered the house. Verbena had drawn a bath for her, complete with flower petals floating in the warm water, and she gratefully sank in.

Up in her bedroom, Zenda dried her hair with a towel and put on a clean nightgown. Then she sat on her bed and took out her journal.

I am not sure what to think about today. Everything is upside down. It feels kind of weird . . . but it feels kind of good, too.

If this is another dimension, I'm not sure I want to leave. Life is so much easier when everyone adores you.

Still, I'd like to find Camille. Why wasn't she at the festival? That really bothers me. I hope I can find her tomorrow.

Zenda closed her journal. Something slipped off the pillowcase and fell into her hand.

It was a flower—a white flower with lacy petals.

"A tempus flower?" Zenda lifted the flower to her nose and smelled the clean scent of snow.

The scent immediately took Zenda's mind back to that afternoon in the clearing when the tempus seeds had swirled around her. Was it a coincidence, or did the tempus flower have something to do with the strange situation she was in?

Just in case, Zenda tucked the flower inside her journal and closed the cover.

But before she put the journal under the pillow, she stopped. Something dawned on her.

The journal might hold some of the answers she was looking for. Zenda slowly opened the cover again. She flipped through the book, stopping at a date the week before. She read the entry.

I am so lucky! When I broke my gazing ball, Verbena and Vetiver wanted me to bind the missing pieces on my own. With no help. Can you believe that?

But the elders stepped in. They are going to try to bind a way to return the pieces of the gazing ball to me. I don't have to do anything. Isn't that great?

I can't wait to tell Alexandra. She knew it all along. Now I can spend more time with her and Gena and Astrid.

—◦◦◦—

Zenda snapped the journal shut. The entry had been written in her handwriting, but she knew she hadn't written those words. This had to be another dimension. She couldn't imagine the elders offering to return her gazing ball to her. And what was all that about Alex and Gena and Astrid?

Reading the entry left Zenda feeling shaken and uneasy. She sank into her bed and drifted off into a restless sleep.

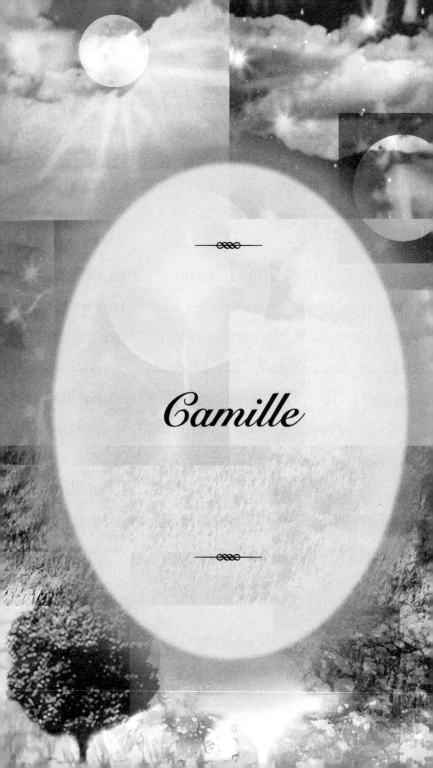

Camille

Zenda woke up early the next morning. Oscar was curled up at her feet. She reached down and picked up the little brown dog. At least some things hadn't changed.

Today was a school day, and Zenda wanted to find Camille before classes began. If this was another dimension, she knew Camille could help her figure it out.

Zenda quickly got dressed and went downstairs to the kitchen. Verbena and Vetiver sat at the table on the screened-in porch, drinking tall glasses of juice and eating muffins.

"You're up early, starshine," Vetiver said. "How did you like the festival yesterday?"

"It was wonderful," Zenda said, grabbing a muffin.

Verbena poured her a glass of pink mango-kiwi juice. "I'm surprised you're up so early," she said.

Zenda swallowed a bite of muffin. "I want to get to school early," she said.

Verbena and Vetiver exchanged glances. Then Verbena pressed her palm against Zenda's forehead.

"Do you think we need to call in the healers?" she asked her husband.

"What do you mean?" Zenda asked. "I feel fine!"

"It's just that you've been acting so strange," Vetiver said. "Zenda, you haven't gone to school in two years."

Zenda felt a strange chill as Vetiver said the words. No school?

"Of course," Zenda said carefully. If Verbena called in the healers, she'd never have a chance to get out and find Camille. "I just meant that I wanted to visit school, to see some of my friends."

"Then you can go at lunchtime," Verbena said. "I don't want the elders to think you're going to classes. They want you here, in the fields, exploring your gift to its fullest."

"I know," Zenda said, even though this

was news to her. So that was it. In her normal world, nobody made a big deal about the fact that she had received her gift of *kani* early. Usually, Alexandra and her friends teased her about it. But in this dimension, everyone seemed to think it was something special.

After breakfast, Zenda wandered into the fields. All signs of the festival had been cleared away. She walked among the rows of flowers and herbs.

Being among the plants made her relax immediately. Zenda stepped into a plot of tall daisies. They leaned toward her as she entered, turning their faces to her as if to say hello.

Zenda smiled. She touched one of the daisy plants and in her mind, asked permission to pick some flowers for her crown. The daisies nodded in response.

Zenda sat in the grass and wove a daisy crown. Their yellow centers nicely matched her pale yellow dress. She leaned back in the grass and stared up at the sun.

If I was at school, I'd be calculating the distance between Azureblue and the nearest planets, or listening to Dr. Ledger drone on and on about seed germination, Zenda realized. Being in the fields was much nicer.

But Zenda soon began to feel lonely. She went back to her room and curled up with Oscar in the cupola, reading a book. She jumped up when she heard the lunch chimes.

She couldn't wait to see Camille. Zenda dashed downstairs and out the door. She waved good-bye to Vetiver, who was pruning roses in the rose garden.

"I'll be back after lunch!" Zenda called.

Zenda took the path to the Commons Circle, which looked the same as it always did. Then she turned down the path to the Cobalt School for Girls.

Zenda was glad to see that the school looked just as she remembered it. Four U-shaped buildings formed a circle around a willow tree. Girls sat in the shade of the tree, eating their lunch on colorful blankets spread on the ground.

Zenda spotted Camille sitting with Sophia, a girl from their class. But before she could reach them, Alex, Gena, and Astrid came up, swarming around her.

"Zenda, it's so great to see you!" Alex beamed. "Come eat lunch with us."

The girls dragged Zenda to an orange blanket. Astrid sat down and immediately handed Zenda a sandwich.

"Take it, Zenda," she said. "I'm not hungry, anyway."

"No, thanks," Zenda said absently. Astrid looked hurt. "I really came to see Camille."

Alexandra burst into giggles, and Gena and Astrid joined her.

"Zenda, you are so funny," Alex said. "Why do you want to see Camille? Do you need to borrow some worms?"

"Or beetles?" Gena said.

"Or maybe some nice ants," Astrid added, giggling again.

Zenda started to get angry. Camille's dream was to be an ethno-entomologist—someone who could communicate with insects the same way Zenda communicated with plants. Zenda always thought Camille's love of bugs was pretty amazing.

"And look who she's sitting with," Alexandra said, leaning closer. "Sophia. Doesn't that girl ever look in a mirror?"

Zenda had always liked Sophia. She almost always wore overalls that were splattered with paint from her art projects. Her curly brown hair never looked combed, and she always used the biggest, brightest flowers for her flower crowns.

"I think Sophia looks nice," Zenda said.

Alexandra frowned. "Zenda, are you feeling all right?"

Zenda stood up. "I'm just fine," she said. "I just don't think it's nice to make fun of Camille and Sophia, that's all."

Zenda marched off and sat on Camille's blanket. Camille and Sophia were eating apples. They stopped in mid-bite when they saw Zenda.

"What do you want?" Sophia asked a little testily.

"Camille, I need to talk to you," Zenda said, ignoring Sophia. "Something strange is happening. You're the only one who will understand. We've been friends for so long."

Camille looked confused. "We were friends when we were little, Zenda," she said. "But you haven't talked to me in ages."

"It's some kind of trick," Sophia said. "Listen, Zenda. Camille and I don't bother you. Why don't you and your little friends just leave us alone?"

Zenda felt sick. Did this mean that she and Camille weren't friends in this dimension?

She couldn't imagine it. Not in a million years.

"Camille, there's something strange going on," she said, trying desperately to explain. "This isn't the way things are supposed to be. It's some kind of crazy dimension. In the real world, you and I are best friends."

Sophia rolled her eyes. "What do you think we are, idiots? Get lost, Zenda."

"Are you sure you're feeling all right?" Camille asked.

Seeing the look of compassion in Camille's eyes, Zenda realized something. Camille hadn't changed at all in this dimension. She was the sweet, nice Cam she had always known.

No. *She* had changed somehow. If she and Camille weren't friends, it was all Zenda's fault.

Zenda stood up. "I'm sorry," she said. "I won't bother you anymore."

Zenda ran away from the willow tree.

She was starting to like this dimension less and less. Without Camille, nothing felt right.

Then Zenda stopped. Mykal stood at the start of the path. He smiled right at her. Zenda felt her stomach flip-flop.

"Your parents told me you were here," he said. "You want to go for a walk?"

A Dream
Come True?

"Sure," Zenda said. "I'll walk with you."

The two walked for a minute in silence. Zenda caught Mykal casting shy glances her way, then turning his head.

Mykal's shyness made her uneasy. She searched her mind for something to talk about. Something that would tell her if this Mykal was the same as her Mykal.

"Hey," Zenda said, brightening suddenly. "Remember that day we were picking stinkbugs off the roses? We were supposed to sneak up on them, but you tripped over a watering can, and the stinkbugs all went off at once?"

She wrinkled her nose. "I'll never forget that smell," she said, laughing. "That was so funny!"

But Mykal didn't laugh. Instead, he looked stricken. "I didn't know you heard about that," he mumbled.

"Of course I heard about it," Zenda replied. "I was there!"

Mykal's green eyes got wide. "You mean you were watching?" He groaned. "How embarrassing!"

"No, I mean I was there," Zenda said. "Picking stinkbugs with you."

That made Mykal smile a little. "You? Picking stinkbugs? You're too . . ." His voice trailed off a little, and he blushed. "I mean, I just can't imagine someone like you picking stinkbugs, that's all."

Zenda's heart skipped a beat. Mykal had never smiled at her like that before.

Mykal walked off the path and sat on a large, flat rock on the bank of Crystal Creek. Zenda sat down next to him.

Being with Mykal felt confusing. The way this Mykal looked at her felt like some kind of dream come true. But he also seemed to think she was some kind of china doll, too fragile to have any fun.

"Come on, Mykal," she said. "Let's go pick some stinkbugs. We'll do it right this time. It'll be fun."

Mykal blushed. "You're so nice," he said. "You'd pick stinkbugs just to be with me."

Mykal looked into Zenda's eyes, and for a moment she forgot everything. It didn't matter that she was in some kind of strange dimension, or that Camille was no longer her friend.

Zenda felt her face flush. She saw Mykal's eyes travel upward, focusing on her flower crown.

Oh, no, Zenda thought. The daisies were probably changing color—or behaving in some other embarrassing way. She quickly reached up to grab the crown. It slipped out of her fingers and fell to the grass at her feet.

"I'll get it," Mykal said quickly.

He and Zenda reached for the crown at the same time. Their hands touched, and for a second, neither one of them let go. Zenda's stomach flip-flopped. She and Mykal had never been this close before. But something didn't feel right.

"I've got to go!" Zenda said, jumping up.

Zenda missed Mykal. The *real* Mykal. Funny, clumsy, plant-obsessed Mykal. Not this Mykal.

Mykal looked confused. "Zenda? What's wrong?"

"I'm sorry," she said.

Then she picked up her crown of daisies and ran back home.

The Second Musing

Zenda flopped onto her bed. She was tired of running. She'd been running from her problems for two days.

Now she wanted some answers.

Zenda picked up Luna and stared into the doll's face.

"I don't know what to do, Luna," she said. "Nothing feels right here. I'm popular. Mykal likes me. I don't have to go to school or do any chores. But I'm not happy at all."

Luna's green eyes smiled at Zenda. She focused on the tiny stitches that formed the doll's eyes. The stitches all blended together, growing fuzzy. In her mind's eye, Zenda saw a swirling blue mist.

The mist evaporated, and Zenda saw her grandmother, Delphina, surrounded by white light. She was sitting on the porch swing, rocking slowly. She had her arm around Zenda, who looked about eight years old.

"I was not a happy child before I

discovered my musings," Delphina was saying. Zenda remembered that day well. She had dropped a potted plant in botany class, sending ceramic shards all over the classroom. Alexandra had called her clumsy, and everyone had laughed.

"Before my musings, I blamed others for making me unhappy," Delphina said. "But that wasn't true. I was unhappy with myself."

The scene faded. Zenda blinked. Delphina's stories all contained gentle lessons. What had her grandmother been trying to tell her?

Zenda thought back to how everything had started. She had been miserable in the nashera patch. She had been afraid to go to the Project Fair because of what Alexandra might do or say. She had definitely been unhappy.

I blamed others for making me unhappy, Delphina had said. *But that wasn't true.*

"But others *were* making me unhappy," Zenda said, looking at Luna. "Verbena and Vetiver made me weed the nashera. And Alexandra says mean things all the time."

As soon as Zenda said the words, she knew the truth.

Her *parents* hadn't made her weed the nashera. She had made that happen by stealing the azura orchid. And Alexandra's mean words were only words; if Zenda hadn't been feeling bad about things already, Alex's teasing wouldn't have bothered her so much.

"That's why I'm not happy here," Zenda said. It wasn't just losing Camille as a friend. "It doesn't matter if people are nice to me or mean to me, or if things go great or get messed up. If I'm not happy with myself, none of that matters."

As soon as Zenda said the words, the faint sound of tinkling bells filled the air. Zenda gasped. She had heard that sound once before.

The air faintly shimmered, as though a shower of tiny specks of gold were falling from the ceiling. Zenda felt something warm in the palm of her hand. She opened it.

A small shard of broken crystal rested there. A pale orange mist swirled around the crystal.

"My second musing," Zenda breathed.

She watched as the mist began to form letters. Soon, the shard was etched with orange writing. Zenda leaned closer to read it.

To find happiness in life, you must first be happy with yourself.

Zenda grinned. For the first time in days, she did feel happy.

"Thank you, Delphina," Zenda whispered.

Back to the Woods

Zenda braced herself. Now that she had found her second musing, she must be headed back to her own dimension. She waited for a light to flash, or some kind of magical portal to appear.

But nothing happened.

"I'm ready to go back to my own dimension now," Zenda announced, although she wasn't sure who—or what—she was supposed to be talking to.

But the only reply she got was a slight breeze blowing through the open window.

Zenda raised her voice. "I said, I'm ready to go back now!"

Verbena walked past the open door. She shook her head. "That's it. I'm contacting the healers. I think you have some kind of fever, Zenda."

Her mother hurried off, and Zenda suddenly felt nervous.

"What if I'm trapped here forever?" Zenda wondered aloud. She picked up Luna again. "Luna, how am I supposed to get back?"

But Luna didn't have the answer, either. Zenda turned over the fragile shard of glass in her hand. She had learned her lesson, and received her musing. What more was there to do?

The crystal shard didn't hold any clues. Zenda remembered the silk pouch around her neck, and tucked the shard inside. As she did, she touched the card she had kept inside.

"Of course," Zenda said out loud. "Persuaja!"

Zenda jumped up and peered down the hallway. It was empty. As she tiptoed down the stairs, she heard Verbena and Vetiver talking in the kitchen.

"She's been acting so strangely," Verbena was saying.

"Don't forget how special she is," Vetiver said. "Perhaps receiving her gift early has consequences we don't know about."

As quietly as she could, Zenda walked down to the front doorway. She made it outside and onto the path without her parents hearing her.

Zenda ran toward the Commons Circle, feeling suddenly free. She'd find Persuaja. She would know what to do. Soon, she'd be back in her own dimension. Back with Camille. Back with Mykal, even if he didn't like her the way she liked him. She couldn't wait.

Zenda ran into the Western Woods and quickly found the stream that led to the Hawthorn Grove. She followed the stream to the circle of thorny trees. Then she walked the circle, trying to remember where she had found the entrance.

Zenda stopped, frowning. She had walked the circle completely, she was sure. But there was no sign of the entrance anywhere.

Zenda walked the circle again.

Then a third time. For some reason, the entrance had closed up.

How am I supposed to get in? Zenda wondered. There were patches in the trees here and there, but it would be a tight squeeze, and she couldn't avoid getting scratched.

Then it came to her. "Of course," she said, feeling foolish. With her gift of *kani*, she could communicate with the trees. It didn't always work the way it was supposed to, but it was worth a try.

Zenda placed her hands lightly against the tree branches. Then she closed her eyes and concentrated.

It was hard to explain to others what *kani* felt like. It wasn't like the plants talked to her, exactly. It was more like she could understand their feelings.

Protect her. Protect her. Protect her.

Zenda opened her eyes, startled. The hawthorns in the grove had closed the opening to protect someone. Did they mean Persuaja?

Zenda remembered the spooky image in the crystal pyramid and shivered.

Zenda tried to tell the plants that she was a friend.

I'm here to help. She concentrated on the words. *I know Persuaja. She is a friend. Please let me in.*

The tree branches began to quiver beneath her fingers. Then they stopped.

Please, Zenda told the trees. *I am not here to harm anyone.*

The branches quivered again, then stopped again.

Zenda stepped back.

"It's no use," she sighed. There had to be some way in without harming the trees.

Then Zenda heard the branches rustle. Slowly, the branches of two of the thorny trees parted to the side, leaving an opening just big enough for her to fit through.

"Thank you!" Zenda said, brushing the leaves with her fingers. "Thank you so much."

Zenda ran through the opening and then stopped abruptly.

Persuaja's cottage had changed. Tangled weeds had overtaken the neat patches of herbs and flowers. The thatched roof looked scraggly, and was marked with holes.

The door was half open, and Zenda stepped into the cottage. The inside was just as messy. Layers of dust covered the purple couch. Many of the hanging herbs had fallen to the floor, their dry leaves breaking into tiny pieces. None of the books were on the shelves, and only a few of the bottles with brightly-colored liquid remained.

"Persuaja?" Zenda called.

She walked through the room to the kitchen. It was pretty much intact, although covered with dust. Zenda turned toward the purple curtains. That's where she had found Persuaja before — but something told her that she would not find her friend there today.

Zenda pushed back the curtains. A hole in the thatched roof above let in a shaft of light which shone directly on the room's small, round table, where Persuaja had been scrying.

"Persuaja," Zenda said, sinking into one of the chairs. "Where are you? What happened?"

As if in answer, a sudden breeze blew through the hole in the roof. Zenda heard a noise and turned around.

There, exactly where it had been before, was Persuaja's crystal pyramid. The velvet cloth draped over it flapped in the breeze.

Zenda stood up and walked to it, then hesitated. The last time she had looked in the crystal, she had seen something horrible.

The breeze blew again, stronger this time, and the velvet cloth slid off the crystal, revealing part of the pyramid.

A white glow came from inside.

Zenda took a deep breath. She had to look. She had to find out what happened to Persuaja. She reached out and removed the black velvet cloth.

Persuaja's face floated in the pyramid.

"Zenda, you're finally here!" she said. "I need your help."

Trapped
in the
Crystal

Zenda went pale. The face in the crystal looked like the vision she had seen in Persuaja's cottage before.

But there was a difference. This Persuaja looked solid and real, not as ghostly as she had in Zenda's vision. It somehow made Zenda feel better.

"Persuaja! What happened?" Zenda asked.

"There is much to tell," Persuaja said. Then she hesitated. "But you are not the Zenda I know, are you?"

Zenda frowned, confused, but then she realized what Persuaja meant. "No, I'm not," she said. "I'm from another dimension. It's a lot like this one . . . but not exactly."

Persuaja nodded. "I understand. But you can still help me. In fact, you may be even more help to me now."

"Persuaja, what happened?" Zenda asked. "Are you stuck in there?"

"I am afraid it is a story you will not enjoy hearing," Persuaja replied.

Zenda wanted more than anything to help her friend. "Please tell me," Zenda said.

"Very well," said Persuaja. "Not long ago, you came to me, asking me to give you information about your future. Your counterpart in this dimension broke her gazing ball, you see."

Zenda flushed. "I know. I did that in my dimension, too."

Persuaja did not seem surprised. "I refused to help. One must discover the mysteries of the gazing ball on one's own. My interference would not have served any purpose."

Persuaja's words sounded familiar to Zenda. Persuaja had said the same thing when Zenda had asked for her help yesterday.

"You were not happy about this," Persuaja continued. "You reported me to the elders, who were persuaded to banish me from the village. I was ready to leave willingly, when I received a vision in my crystal. A vision that you were in trouble and needed my help. I did not know then, of course, that the Zenda in trouble was from another dimension."

Zenda felt terrible. The more she heard, the more she did not like the Zenda who lived in this dimension. How could she have demanded that Persuaja be banished?

"I needed a place to hide, so I transported myself inside the pyramid," Persuaja went on. "I planned to return when you entered this dimension. I sensed the dimensional shift yesterday, but I have not been able to leave the crystal as I should."

"Why not?" Zenda asked.

Persuaja's face clouded. "The gift of a psychic is not always understood. Many fear it. It is possible that one of the elders put some kind of seal on the cottage to prevent me from returning. The energy of the pyramid must be unsealed in order for me to leave."

"I'll do it!" Zenda said. She had to fix things, somehow. "Just tell me what to do."

"Do you know the gortberry bush?" Persuaja asked.

Zenda nodded. They grew wild in the woods. When the yellow berries were in season, she often went on berry-picking expeditions with her father and mother. They used them in healing potions.

"Find me a cluster of ripe gortberries and bring them here as quickly as you can," Persuaja instructed. "There is a potion that can be made that will release the seal."

Zenda turned to leave, then stopped. It didn't feel right leaving Persuaja all by herself.

"Will you be all right?" she asked.

"The trees in the grove have protected me for this long," Persuaja replied. "I will be fine."

Zenda left the cottage and exited the grove. Without even asking, the trees parted their branches for her once again.

"Thank you," Zenda told them.

99

She scanned the woods, deciding on a course of action.

The last time she had picked gortberries was two years ago, and she wasn't sure where they grew. She closed her eyes, trying to remember. She and Verbena and Vetiver had walked along the stream, then branched off onto some kind of trail. She remembered going over a bridge, too.

Zenda walked back down the stream, looking for the trail. The air smelled damp, and she could see dark clouds forming through the gaps in the treetops, plunging the woods into darkness.

Zenda would have given anything for a moonglow flower to light the way, but she knew the vines could not grow in the shady woods. But her eyes gradually adjusted to the darkness, and soon she saw it: a space between two trees, the entrance of a trail that had been tramped down and cleared by gortberry pickers over the years.

Zenda started on the path. Normally, her *kani* caused her to pick up on the energy of plants as she passed by. These trees seemed to be very, very old, and very, very quiet, as though they were in the middle of a long nap. The stillness was unnerving rather than soothing.

Gortberry bushes grew low to the ground, so Zenda kept her sights low. But there were no bushes in sight.

I think I have to go over the bridge first, Zenda thought, trying to remember. She looked down the trail, but didn't see anything that looked like a bridge.

Zenda took a few more steps. Then suddenly, she stopped, her heart pounding.

She had arrived at the bridge—or at least, where the bridge should have been. In the dim light, Zenda could make out a few broken wooden planks dangling from ropes over the edge of a ravine.

Zenda had almost stepped into the

ravine, a deep trench carved into the earth. She took a careful step backward and looked down.

The ravine was too wide to jump across. The sides of the ravine sloped steeply to the bottom. It would be a tough climb.

Zenda searched for a way to get across. The ropes of the broken bridge were tied securely to two wooden posts on her side of the ravine. She tugged on a rope, and it seemed solid enough.

Years of running around the village with Mykal and Camille, climbing rocks and scaling walls, were a help to her now. She gripped the rope tightly and made her way down the steep slope.

Dry earth crunched beneath her feet as she walked across the bottom of the ravine to the other side. She looked up at the tall, smooth wall of dirt in front of her. There was no rope on this side, and no jutting rocks or crevices to grab onto if she climbed.

All she could see was a tangle of vines dangling over the edge, out of reach.

Zenda kicked the dirt wall. It wasn't fair! She was so close to the gortberries, but there was no way to get them.

But she had to do it. Without the gortberries, Persuaja would be trapped inside the crystal pyramid forever.

And Zenda would never get home.

Vines and
Gortberries

Zenda tried not to panic. She closed her eyes and took ten slow, deep breaths.

Zenda opened her eyes. She felt calmer, more in control. She surveyed the scene again. There had to be some way up— some way she hadn't thought of.

But all she could see were the vines. And they were too high to do any good.

Or maybe they weren't . . .

Her *kani* had helped her enter the Hawthorn Grove. Maybe it could help her now.

She stood on her toes and reached up toward the vines, stretching her fingers. Then she closed her eyes and called out to the vines with her mind.

Please help me, she asked them. *Please come closer. I have to get up to the gortberries.*

The vines responded more quickly than the hawthorn trees had. One of the vines arched up, as though it was listening to her.

Then it slowly extended down the side of the ditch, slithering like a snake.

"Thank you," Zenda said gratefully. She reached out and grabbed the vine, giving it a tug. It felt solidly grounded.

Probably wrapped around a tree trunk, Zenda guessed. She wrapped both hands around the vine and began to climb. She quickly reached the top of the ditch. Then she set down the vines, thanked them again, and found herself on the edge of the gortberry patch.

The compact shrubs had shiny green leaves and bore clusters of small, white berries. Zenda frowned. Persuaja had asked for ripe berries, but these berries were a few days shy of ripe. Properly ripe gortberries were the bright yellow color of a canary.

Zenda scanned the patch for ripe berries, but found none. The branches rustled as she walked past, sensing her anxiety.

She shook her head at the rustling

branches. The answer was obvious. Kneeling down, she placed her hands on a clump of berries.

The berries' energy was bright and bursting with life. Zenda closed her eyes, focusing all of her concentration on her hands. Getting tree branches to part and vines to move was one thing, but could she really coax berries into ripeness? There was only one way to find out.

As Zenda focused, she felt the *kani* energy flow through her palms like warm honey. It was like nothing she had ever felt before. In the back of her mind, she remembered her mother and father telling her that the *kani* would be easier to control the more she practiced. She hadn't listened to them before, but now she understood.

Not only did her palms feel warm, but she felt a warmth coming from the berries, too. Zenda opened her eyes and watched, transfixed, as the white berries took on a yellow glow. Soon, they glowed as brightly as sunshine among the dark green leaves.

"I'm going to pick you now," Zenda told the gortberries. "Persuaja needs you."

The clump of berries came off easily in her hand. Zenda felt a surge of pride.

She left the gortberry patch, climbed down and back up the ravine once more, and then ran back to Persuaja's cottage as fast as she could. Persuaja's dark eyes shone when she saw Zenda.

"Excellent!" she said. "And now for the potion."

Zenda had seen her parents at work in their greenhouse lab before, but she had never helped. It had all seemed so complicated. Persuaja's potion was no different.

Following Persuaja's instructions, Zenda searched the drawers and shelves in the near-empty cottage and came up with a small iron pot, a thick beeswax candle, a few stems of dried rosemary, and a glass bottle of thick, golden liquid with a cork stopper. Then she fetched some clean water from the well in back of the cottage.

The potion had to boil, so Zenda carefully picked up the crystal pyramid and moved it next to the fireplace so Persuaja could oversee the potion-making. Zenda held her breath with each step. Just thinking about dropping the crystal made her palms damp with sweat.

But she set down the pyramid without breaking it. Then she got to work. She lit the candle in the bottom of the fireplace and hung the pot over it. Then she filled the pot with water and waited for it to boil.

It took a long time, and Zenda watched the woods grow darker and darker outside the cottage. It was almost nighttime. Zenda absently wondered if Verbena and Vetiver were worried about her—and then suddenly remembered her parents, back in her own dimension.

"I've got to get back home," Zenda

said, starting to panic just as the water in the pot began to bubble. "I've been gone so long. Verbena and Vetiver must think I've disappeared or something!"

"You will return soon," Persuaja said. "I will help you. But first, I must get out of here. I believe the water is boiling now."

Persuaja was right. Zenda followed Persuaja's careful instructions and added the rosemary, the cluster of gortberries, plucked from the stem, and finally the entire contents of the bottle of gold liquid.

"What is it?" Zenda asked, pouring it into the pot.

Persuaja smiled. "I can't give away all my secrets now, can I? Now we must let the potion boil."

Zenda waited in silence with Persuaja for what seemed like an eternity. Zenda's very first musing popped into her mind.

Every flower blooms in its own time.

That musing had appeared to teach her

a lesson about impatience. It wasn't an easy lesson to remember, but Zenda had tried.

Finally, the psychic announced it was time to remove the potion from the fire.

"Carefully, now," Persuaja said. "Don't spill a drop. We must let it cool a bit first."

They waited some more. *No wonder Verbena and Vetiver are always working*, Zenda realized. *This takes forever!*

"It's ready," Persuaja said out of the blue. "Pick up the pyramid. Lower it carefully into the potion. Then stand back!"

Zenda picked up the crystal pyramid, suddenly feeling nervous. What if she had done something wrong? What if the potion didn't work? She thought back to the vision she saw back in her own dimension . . .

"Persuaja, I need to tell you something," Zenda began.

"Your vision is not what you think it is," Persuaja said quickly. "Now, into the potion. Hurry!"

How did Persuaja know what she had been thinking? Something in the psychic's voice told her not to ask. She lowered the pyramid into the potion and stepped back.

The ear-splitting sound of shattering glass came from the pot. A blinding yellow light filled the cottage.

Then everything went black.

No Place Like Home

"Persuaja?" Zenda called out. A feeling of dread came over her. If something happened to Persuaja, it would be all her fault.

But the darkness slowly evaporated, revealing Persuaja standing in the center of the room. Her dark eyes flashed.

"Well done!" Persuaja said, and her voice seemed to fill every corner of the cottage. Zenda could not imagine that this larger-than-life woman had been trapped inside the pyramid.

Persuaja stepped over shards of the broken crystal scattered around her black boots.

"A good crystal pyramid is hard to find," she sighed, shaking her head. "But it had to be done."

Zenda wanted to run up and give her a hug, but something about Persuaja held her back. It was like she had an invisible barrier around her, separating her from the rest of the world. It didn't feel magical—just like

Persuaja didn't want anyone to get too close.

"I'm so glad it worked," Zenda said.

"And now we must work on your problem," Persuaja said. "Tell me, have you been in the presence of any tempus flowers recently?"

Zenda nodded. "I think that's how I got here," she said. "Some tempus seeds blew into the village. Then they sprouted and starting growing really quickly. When the flowers bloomed, I started to feel sleepy. Then I woke up in this dimension."

"Of course that's how you got here," Persuaja said. "I don't know what kind of dimension you come from, where tempus seeds are allowed to go flying around unguarded. We keep ours under lock and key here."

Then she frowned. "Of course, that's our problem."

"What do you mean?" Zenda asked.

"We need tempus flowers to return you

to your dimension," Persuaja said. "I suppose I could petition the elders, but it wouldn't be easy."

Zenda remembered the flower she had found on her pillow. "I know where we can get a tempus flower," she said. She told Persuaja about the flower she had tucked in her journal.

Persuaja raised an eyebrow. "One flower? It may be possible. Of course, I'd have to increase the potency . . ." Her voice trailed off for a moment. Then she abruptly nodded at Zenda. "Go get it, then! I'll get things ready here."

Night had fallen, leaving the woods completely dark. Luckily, Zenda was able to follow the sound of the bubbling stream all the way back to the path. As soon as she reached the Commons Circle, she found some moon-glow vines growing wild and plucked a blossom. The glowing white flower lit the way home.

As she approached the house, Zenda

saw shadows through the front windows. She tucked the moonglow flower into the pocket of her dress and quietly walked up to the side window, keeping out of sight.

Through the glass, she could see Vetiver pacing the floor of the sitting room. Verbena was sitting in a chair across from someone in a blue robe.

A healer. Verbena had said she would call in a healer for Zenda. And Zenda had been missing for hours. They must be in a panic.

Zenda tried to think. She just needed to get a tempus flower and go home. There had to be a way to do that without being seen.

Zenda walked to the back of the house and looked up at her bedroom window. Right underneath it, a trellis overgrown with morning glories rested against the house.

She carefully stepped on the first rung of the trellis, testing her weight. The trellis held steady. She climbed up, trying to avoid stepping on the morning glory flowers. Then she shimmied through her window.

Oscar jumped off the green velvet chair when he saw her, wagging his tail. Zenda put a finger to her lips and gently patted his head. She could hear the worried voices of her parents coming from downstairs. As quietly as she could, she slid the journal out from under her pillow and removed the tempus flower.

"Bye, Oscar," she whispered. "I'll see you soon."

Then she climbed back down the trellis.

When she arrived at Persuaja's cottage, the psychic was seated at the kitchen table, holding a glass vial of clear liquid.

"Do you have the flower?" Persuaja asked.

Zenda handed her the tempus flower.

"Excellent," Persuaja said. She dropped the flower into the vial. "It should be ready in just a minute."

"Thank you so much," Zenda said. She hesitated. She had something to tell Persuaja before she left.

"The me—I mean, the Zenda that you know. I'm sorry she made the elders banish you," Zenda said. "What will you do now?"

Persuaja smiled. "Azureblue is filled with many villages, Zenda. I will find a village where I am needed."

"Thank you," Zenda said. "Thanks for staying to save me. If you hadn't waited in the pyramid for me, I'd be stuck here forever."

"And that, my dear, is what psychics do," she said. She picked up the vial. "It's ready!"

"Do I drink it?" Zenda asked, wrinkling her nose.

"Breathe, Zenda," Persuaja said. "Just breathe."

Persuaja held the vial under Zenda's nose. The familiar smell of fallen snow overwhelmed her, just as it had in the Western Woods. Her eyelids drooped. She felt her body falling to the floor . . .

Images swirled in her mind. Little girls in lavender dresses danced, moving like butterflies through her vision. Alexandra handed her a crown of bright red flowers. Camille walked away from her, turning back to look at her sadly. Mykal reached out his hand . . . and then ran off after a flying stinkbug.

And then she saw Persuaja's face, her dark eyes glittering one second, and her face breaking into pieces the next, like the shards of the crystal pyramid . . .

Zenda woke up suddenly, her heart beating wildly. She was back in the clearing of tempus flowers. The snow-white blossoms had all turned brown and drooped on their stems.

Zenda jumped to her feet. It worked! She was back in her own dimension . . . or, at least she hoped she was. She ran back to

120

Persuaja's cottage.

She found Persuaja standing in front of her door, a look of concern on her face.

"Zenda, where have you been?" she asked. "Something has happened with the tempus seeds. I can feel it. They've planted themselves. It isn't safe out there."

"How long have I been gone?" Zenda asked.

"Not more than a few minutes," Persuaja said, her eyes focusing on Zenda's. She raised an eyebrow. "Or have you? Zenda, I think you have a story to tell me."

"I do," Zenda admitted. She told Persuaja everything, from her vision in the crystal pyramid to the vial that had brought her back. Persuaja smiled when Zenda told her how her counterpart in the other dimension had hidden herself in the pyramid.

"How interesting," she said. "I've always wanted to try that."

"So am I really back?" Zenda asked

when she had finished the story. "I mean, how can I be sure?"

"The power of the tempus flower is very specific," Persuaja said. "Anyone who inhales enough of it is transported into a dimension of her own creation. If you truly wanted to come home again, then you are in the right place, Zenda."

Zenda sighed with relief. She hoped Persuaja was right. But she knew deep down that she wouldn't be sure until she found her friends and family again.

"Take me to the tempus flowers before you go," Persuaja said. "I must contain them before they reseed."

Zenda led Persuaja back to the clearing.

"I'm sorry all this happened," she told Persuaja. "I got really scared when I saw that vision of you in the pyramid. But it must have been showing me a vision of you in the other dimension."

"Perhaps," Persuaja said. Her voice sounded uneasy.

"But I shouldn't have looked at the pyramid in the first place," Zenda said. "You were right. I needed to go to that dimension to find my second musing. I needed to experience it for myself. Otherwise, I never would have understood it."

Persuaja stopped. "Do you really think so?" she asked.

Zenda nodded. "I do."

To Zenda's amazement, the sound of bells filled the air in the woods. Another shard of crystal appeared in her palm. This time, purple mist swirled around the circle. Zenda and Persuaja watched together as the mist formed words in the shard.

The best thing about the future is that it happens one day at a time.

Zenda softly whispered the words. Of course. She had wanted Persuaja to give her a shortcut to her future. But she had to

123

experience it herself to really understand it. That's what the musing meant. It was the journey to the future—one day at a time—that was really important.

"My third musing," Zenda said, her voice rising with excitement. "I can't believe it!"

Persuaja smiled. "Even I did not predict that!"

Back
to Normal

When Zenda got home, she found her parents sitting on the porch with Mari, the village elder. Zenda sighed.

I must be back in the right dimension, she thought. *I'm right back in trouble.*

Zenda steeled herself and walked up onto the porch.

"I guess you know what happened," she said.

"I told them," Mari said gently. "And I must say, I'm disappointed in you, Zenda."

Zenda looked away. "I know. I'm sorry I made those firebrush flowers go off."

"Oh dear, no," Mari said, shaking her head. "You couldn't help that. I'm disappointed that you ran away."

The comment took Zenda by surprise.

"No one expects you to be able to handle your gift, Zenda," Mari continued. "That will come with time and practice. But you shouldn't let what others think matter to you so much. Your grandmother, Delphina,

126

would not have run. She would have stayed and enjoyed the fair."

Zenda knew she was right. Her second musing came to mind.

To find happiness in life, you must first be happy with yourself.

Relief swept over Zenda. She wasn't in trouble for setting off the firebrush flowers. The elders didn't think she was some kind of freak.

She smiled. "I know," she said. "I shouldn't have run."

"We were worried about you," Verbena said, giving her a hug. "Where did you go?"

"It's a long story," Zenda said. She opened the pouch around her neck. "But it has a happy ending."

Zenda shook the two shards of her gazing ball onto her hand. Verbena gasped with delight.

"Two more musings!" she cried.

"You must have had quite a day, starshine," Vetiver said.

You can say that again, Zenda thought.

Mari picked up one of the musings and examined it. "Fascinating," she said. "You must come talk to me of your experiences sometime, Zenda. I think the elders would find them very useful."

"I will," Zenda said.

Mari hugged her tightly, and for a second Zenda felt like she was in her grandmother's arms again. She felt sad to see Mari head back down the path.

"I've got more good news for you," Vetiver said. "We made plans today for your school break. How would you like to go to Crystallin?"

Zenda shrieked happily. She hugged Vetiver, then Verbena.

"Are we really going?" she asked.

Since she was a child, Zenda had dreamed of visiting one of the other planets in the solar system. But she had never left Azureblue.

Vetiver nodded. "Yes, we are," he said. "We'll be staying with your cousins."

Zenda felt like dancing. Oscar ran out the door, wagging his tail. She picked him up and twirled him around the porch.

Zenda felt happy—but something was missing.

"I'm going to go back to the fair," she said. "Is that okay?"

Her parents looked at each other and smiled.

"Have a good time, starshine," Vetiver said. "We'll see you at supper."

Zenda ran all the way to the Cobalt School for Boys. Although Zenda had been gone for days, only an hour or so had passed in this dimension. The Maple Building was still crowded with elders, boys, and girls, talking and looking at the projects.

Alex, Gena, and Astrid stood by the

front door. Alexandra raised her eyebrows when she saw Zenda approach.

"Better call the Fire Squad," she announced loudly. "Zenda's back!"

Astrid and Gena burst into giggles.

"Don't you have anything better to do, Alex?" Zenda asked her. "I know I do."

Alex looked stunned. Zenda swept by the girls. There was someone she had to find.

"Camille!" Zenda shouted. She pushed through the crowd and wrapped her arms around Camille's neck.

"Zenda, are you all right?" Camille asked. "I was so worried about you."

"I have so much to tell you," Zenda said. "But mostly, I need to tell you that I think you're the best friend in the whole world."

"Thanks," Camille said, looking slightly startled. "You are, too."

Zenda felt a tap on her shoulder. She turned around to see Sophia. Zenda froze for a second, remembering their unfriendly encounter in the other dimension.

"I love what you did with those firebrush flowers," Sophia said. "It was really wild."

"Thanks," Zenda said. "But I didn't really mean to do it. It was an accident."

"Accidents happen."

Zenda turned. Mykal stood next to her, smiling.

"I always thought the Project Fair could use some fireworks," he said. "It's pretty boring, if you ask me."

Relief washed over Zenda. The boy standing next to her was the Mykal she remembered. But just to be sure . . .

"Feel like picking some stinkbugs with me tomorrow?" she asked.

"Sure," Mykal said eagerly. "Since that last time, I've been working on a new method for capturing them. I created a spray out of rose essence that we can use to lure them away from the plants . . ."

I almost wish I hadn't asked Mykal about the stinkbugs. He went on forever about stinkbugs and natural repellents. Of course, Camille stood up for the stinkbugs. And now I'm stuck picking stinkbugs tomorrow, plus I've got to finish weeding the nashera patch.

Which all means that I'm in the right place. And it feels good.

I'm even starting to feel better about my kani. It felt amazing to watch those gortberries ripen in front of my eyes. Maybe if I keep practicing, I'll be able to control things better.

And the best thing of all is that I'm going to Crystallin! They call it the

Crystal Planet. On a clear night, you can see Crystallin shining in the sky. When I was little, I used to make wishes on it.

I can see it shining through my window right now. Maybe I should make a wish . . .

I wish that I'll find another one of my musings on Crystallin. I already bound three musings, and I have ten more to go. That seems like a lot.

But I've already bound one musing in another dimension. Who knows what I'll bind on another planet!

Cosmically yours,
Zenda